A Thorny Path

Volume 05

Georg Ebers

(Translator: Clara Bell)

Alpha Editions

This edition published in 2023

ISBN : 9789357947237

Design and Setting By
Alpha Editions
www.alphaedis.com
Email - info@alphaedis.com

Contents

VOLUME 5.

CHAPTER XV.

Nothing delighted old Dido more than to dress the daughter of her beloved mistress in all her best, for she had helped to bring her up; but to-day it was a cruel task; tears dimmed her old eyes. It was not till she had put the finishing touches to braiding the girl's abundant brown hair, pinned her peplos on the shoulders with brooches, and set the girdle straight, that her face cleared, as she looked at the result. Never had she seen her darling look so fair. Nothing, indeed, remained of the child-like timidity and patient submissiveness which had touched Dido only two days since, as she plaited Melissa's hair. The maiden's brow was grave and thoughtful, the lips firmly set; but she seemed to Dido to have grown, and to have gained something of her mother's mature dignity. She looked, the old woman told her, like the image of Pallas Athene; adding, to make her smile, that if she wanted an owl, she, Dido, could fill the part. Jesting had never been the old woman's strong point, and to-day it was less easy than ever; for, if the worst befell, and she were sent in her old age to a strange house—and Argutis, no doubt, to another—she would have to turn the handmill for the rest of her days.

But it was a hard task which the motherless—and now fatherless—girl had set herself, and she must try to cheer her darling. While she was dressing her, she never ceased praying to all the gods and goddesses she could think of to come to the maiden's aid and move the souls of those who could help her. And though she was, as a rule, ready to expect the worst, this time she hoped for the best; for Seleukus's wife must have a heart of stone if she could close it to such innocence, such beauty, and the pathetic glance of those large, imploring eyes.

When at length Melissa quitted the house, deeply veiled, with Argutis to escort her, she took his arm; and he, wearing his master's mantle, and exempted long since from keeping his hair cropped, was so proud of this that he walked with all the dignity of a freeman, and no one could have guessed that he was a slave. Melissa's face was completely hidden, and she, like her companion, was safe from recognition. Argutis, nevertheless, led her through the quietest and darkest lanes to the Kanopic way. Both were silent, and looked straight before them. Melissa, as she walked on, could not think with her usual calm. Like a suffering man who goes to the physician's house to die or be cured by the knife, she felt that she was on her way to something terrible in itself, to remedy, if possible, something still more dreadful. Her father— Alexander, so reckless and so good-hearted—Philip, whom she pitied—and her sick lover, came in turn before her fancy. But she could not control her mind to dwell on either for long. Nor could she, as usual, when she had any serious purpose in hand, put up a prayer to her mother's manes or the immortals; and all the while an inner voice made itself heard, confidently promising her that Caesar, for whom she had sacrificed, and who might be kinder and more merciful than others fancied, would at once grant all she should ask. But she would not listen; and when she nevertheless ventured to consider how she could make her way into Caesar's presence, a cold shiver ran down her back, and again Philip's last words sounded in her ears, "Death rather than dishonor!"

Other thoughts and feelings filled the slave's soul. He, who had always watched over his master's children with far more anxious care than Heron himself, had not said a word to dissuade Melissa from her perilous expedition. Her plan had, indeed, seemed to him the only one which promised any success. He was a man of sixty years, and a shrewd fellow, who might easily have found a better master than Heron had been; but he gave not a thought to his own prospects—only to Melissa's, whom he loved as a child of his own. She had placed herself under his protection, and he felt responsible for her fate. Thus he regarded it as great good fortune that he could be of use in procuring her admission to the house of Seleukus, for the door-keeper was a fellow-countryman of his, whom Fate had brought hither from the banks of the Moselle. At every festival, which secured a few hours' liberty to all the slaves, they had for years been boon companions, and Argutis knew that his friend would do for him and his young mistress all that lay in his power. It would, of course, be difficult to get an audience of the mistress of a house where Caesar was a guest, but the door-keeper was clever and ingenious, and would do anything short of the impossible.

So he walked with his head high and his heart full of pride, and it confirmed his courage when one of Zminis's men, whom they passed in the brightly illuminated Kanopic street, and who had helped to secure Philip, looked at him without recognizing him.

There was a great stir in this, the handsomest road through the city. The people were waiting for Caesar; but stricter order was observed than on the occasion of his arrival. The guard prohibited all traffic on the southern side of the way, and only allowed the citizens to walk up and down the footpath, shaded by trees, between the two roadways paved with granite flags, and the arcades in front of the houses on either side. The free inhabitants, unaccustomed to such restrictions, revenged themselves by cutting witticisms at Caesar's expense, "for clearing the streets of Alexandria by his men-at-arms as he did those of Rome by the executioner. He seemed to have forgotten, as he kept the two roads open, that he only needed one, now that he had murdered his brother and partner."

Melissa and her companion were ordered to join the crowd on the footway; but Argutis managed to convince a man on guard that they were two of the mimes who were to perform before Caesar—the door-keeper at the house of Seleukus would confirm the fact—and the official himself made way for them into the vestibule of this splendid dwelling.

But Melissa was as little in the humor to admire all the lavish magnificence which surrounded her as Alexander had been a few days since. Still veiled, she modestly took a place among the choir who stood on each side of the hall ready to welcome Caesar with singing and music. Argutis stopped to speak with his friend. She dimly felt that the whispering and giggling all about her was at her expense; and when an elderly, man, the choir-master, asked her what she wanted, and desired her to remove her veil, she obeyed at once, saying: "Pray let me stand here, the Lady Berenike will send for me."

"Very well," replied the musician; and he silenced the singers, who were hazarding various impertinent guesses as to the arrival of so pretty a girl just when Caesar was expected.

As Melissa dropped her veil the splendor of the scene, lighted up by numberless tapers and lamps, forced itself on her attention. She now perceived that the porphyry columns of the great hall were wreathed with flowers, and that garlands swung in graceful curves from the open roof; while at the farther end, statues had been placed of Septimus Severus and Julia Domna, Caracalla's parents. On each side of these works of art stood bowers of plants, in which gay-plumaged birds were fluttering about, excited by the lights. But all these glories swam before her eyes, and the first question which the artist's daughter was wont to ask herself, "is it really beautiful or no?" never occurred to her mind. She did not even notice the smell of incense, until some fresh powder was thrown on, and it became oppressive.

She was fully conscious only of two facts, when at last Argutis returned: that she was the object of much curious examination and that every one was wondering what detained Caesar so long.

At last, after she had waited many long minutes, the door-keeper approached her with a young woman in a rich but simple dress, in whom she recognized Johanna, the Christian waiting-maid of whom Alexander had spoken. She did not speak, but beckoned her to come.

Breathing anxiously, and bending her head low, Melissa, following her guide, reached a handsome impluvium, where a fountain played in the midst of a bed of roses. Here the moon and starlight mingled with that of lamps without number, and the ruddy glare of a blaze; for all round the basin, from which the playing waters danced skyward, stood marble genii, carrying in their hands or on their heads silver dishes, in which the leaping flames consumed cedar chips and aromatic resins.

At the back of this court, where it was as light as day, at the top of three steps, stood the statues of Alexander the Great and Caracalla. They were of equal size; and the artist, who had wrought the second in great haste out of the slightest materials, had been enjoined to make Caesar as like as possible in every respect to the hero he most revered. Thus they looked like brothers. The figures were lighted up by the fires which burned on two altars of ivory and gold. Beautiful boys, dressed as armed Erotes, fed the flames.

The whole effect was magical and bewildering; but, as she followed her guide, Melissa only felt that she was in the midst of a new world, such as she might perhaps have seen in a dream; till, as they passed the fountain, the cool drops sprinkled her face.

Then she suddenly remembered what had brought her hither. In a minute she must appear as a supplicant in the presence of Korinna's mother—perhaps even in that of Caesar himself—and the fate of all dear to her depended on her demeanor. The sense of fulfilling a serious duty was uppermost in her mind. She drew herself up, and replaced a stray lock of hair; and her heart beat almost to bursting as she saw a number of, men standing on the platform at the top of the steps, round a lady who had just risen from her ivory seat. Giving her hand to a Roman senator, distinguished by the purple edge to his toga, she descended the steps, and advanced to meet Melissa.

This dignified matron, who was awaiting the ruler of the world and yet could condescend to come forward to meet a humble artist's daughter, was taller by half a head than her illustrious companion; and the few minutes during which Berenike was coming toward her were enough to fill Melissa with thankfulness, confidence, and admiration. And even in that short time, as she gazed at the magnificent dress of blue brocade shot with gold and sparkling with precious stones which draped the lady's majestic figure, she thought how keen a pang it must cost the mother, so lately bereft of her only child, to maintain a kindly, nay, a genial aspect, in the midst of this display, toward Caesar and a troop of noisy guests.

The sincerest pity for this woman, rich and preeminent as she was, filled the soul of the girl, who herself was so much to be pitied. But when the lady had come up to her, and asked, in her deep voice, what was the danger that threatened her brother, Melissa, with unembarrassed grace, and although it was the first time she had ever addressed a lady of such high degree, answered simply, with a full sense of the business in hand:

"My name is Melissa; I am the sister of Alexander the painter. I know it is overbold to venture into your presence just now, when you have so much else to think of; but I saw no other way of saving my brother's life, which is in peril."

At this Berenike seemed surprised. She turned to her companion, who was her sister's husband, and the first Egyptian who had been admitted to the Roman Senate, and said, in a tone of gentle reproach:

"Did not I say so, Coeranus? Nothing but the most urgent need would have brought Alexander's sister to speak with me at such an hour."

And the senator, whose black eyes had rested with pleasure on Melissa's rare beauty, promptly replied, "And if she had come for the veriest trifle she would be no less welcome to me."

"Let me hear no more of such speeches," Berenike exclaimed with some annoyance.—"Now, my child, be quick. What about your brother?"

Melissa briefly and truthfully reported Alexander's heedless crime and the results to her father and Philip. She ended by beseeching the noble lady with fervent pathos to intercede for her father and brothers.

Meanwhile the senator's keen face had darkened, and the lady Berenike's large eyes, too, were downcast. She evidently found it hard to come to a decision; and for the moment she was relieved of the necessity, for runners came hurrying up, and the senator hastily desired Melissa to stand aside.

He whispered to his sister-in-law:

"It will never do to spoil Caesar's good-humor under your roof for the sake of such people," and Berenike had only time to reply, "I am not afraid of him," when the messenger explained to her that Caesar himself was prevented from coming, but that his representatives, charged with his apologies, were close at hand.

On this Coeranus exclaimed, with a sour smile: "Admit that I am a true prophet! You have to put up with the same treatment that we senators have often suffered under."

But the matron scarcely heard him. She cast her eyes up to heaven with sincere thanksgiving as she murmured with a sigh of relief, "For this mercy the gods be praised!"

She unclasped her hands from her heaving bosom, and said to the steward who had followed the messengers:

"Caesar will not be present. Inform your lord, but so that no one else may hear. He must come here and receive the imperial representatives with me. Then have my couch quietly removed and the banquet served at once. O Coeranus, you can not imagine the misery I am thus spared!"

"Berenike!" said the senator, in a warning voice, and he laid his finger on his lips. Then turning to the young supplicant, he said to her in a tone of regret:

"So your walk is for nothing, fair maid. If you are as sensible as you are pretty, you will understand that it is too much to ask any one to stand between the lion and the prey which has roused his ire."

The lady, however, did not heed the caution which her brother-in-law intended to convey. As Melissa's imploring eyes met her own, she said, with clear decision:

"Wait here. We shall see who it is that Caesar sends. I know better than my lord here what it is to see those dear to us in peril. How old are you, child?"

"Eighteen," replied Melissa.

"Eighteen?" repeated Berenike, as if the word were a pain to her, for her daughter had been just of that age. Then she said, louder and with encouraging kindness:

"All that lies in my power shall be done for you and yours.—And you, Coeranus, must help me."

"If I can," he replied, "with all the zeal of my reverence for you and my admiration for beauty. But here come the envoys. The elder, I see, is our learned Philostratus, whose works are known to you; the younger is Theocritus, the favorite of fortune of whom I was telling you. If the charm of that face might but conquer the omnipotent youth—"

"Coeranus!" she exclaimed, with stern reproof; but she failed to hear the senator's excuses, for her husband, Seleukus, followed her down the steps, and with a hasty sign to her, advanced to meet his guests.

Theocritus was spokesman, and notwithstanding the mourning toga which wrapped him in fine folds, his gestures did not belie his origin as an actor and dancer. When Seleukus presented him to his wife, Theocritus assured her that when, but an hour since, his sovereign lord, who was already dressed and wreathed for the banquet, had learned that the gods had bereft of their only child the couple whose hospitality had promised him such a delightful evening, he had been equally shocked and grieved. Caesar was deeply distressed at the unfortunate circumstance that he should have happened in his ignorance to intrude on the seclusion which was the prerogative of grief. He begged to assure her and her husband of the high favor of the ruler of the world. As for himself, Theocritus, he would not fail to describe the splendor with which they had decorated their princely residence in Caesar's honor. His imperial master would be touched, indeed, to hear that even the bereaved mother, who, like Niobe, mourned for her offspring, had broken the stony spell which held her to Sipylos, and had decked herself to receive the greatest of all earthly guests as radiant as Juno at the golden table of the gods.

The lady succeeded in controlling herself and listening to the end of these pompous phrases without interrupting the speaker. Every word which flowed so glibly from his tongue fell on her ear as bitter mockery; and he himself was so repugnant to her, that she felt it a release when, after exchanging a few words with the master of the house, he begged leave to retire, as important business called him away. And this, indeed, was the truth. For no consideration would he have left this duty to another, for it was to communicate to Titianus, who had offended him, the intelligence that Caesar had deprived him of the office of prefect, and intended to examine into certain complaints of his administration.

The second envoy, however, remained, though he refused Seleukus's invitation to fill his place at the banquet. He exchanged a few words with the lady Berenike, and presently found himself taken aside by the senator, and, after a short explanation, led up to Melissa, whom Coeranus desired to appeal for help to Philostratus, the famous philosopher, who enjoyed Caesar's closest confidence.

Coeranus then obeyed a sign from Berenike, who wished to know whether he would be answerable for introducing this rarely pretty girl, who had placed herself under their protection—and whom she, for her part, meant to protect—to a courtier of whom she knew nothing but that he was a writer of taste.

The question seemed to amuse Coeranus, but, seeing that his sister-in-law was very much in earnest, he dropped his flippant tone and admitted that Philostratus, as a young man, had been one of the last with whom he would trust a girl. His far-famed letters sufficiently proved that the witty philosopher had been a devoted and successful courtier of women. But that was all a thing of the past. He still, no doubt, did homage to female beauty, but he led a regular life, and had become one of the most ardent and earnest upholders of religion and virtue. He was one of the learned circle which gathered round Julia Domna, and it was by her desire that he had accompanied Caracalla, to keep his mad passions in check when it might be possible.

The conversation between Melissa and the philosopher had meanwhile taken an unexpected turn. At his very first address the reply had died on her lips, for in Caesar's representative she had recognized the Roman whom she had seen in the Temple of Asklepios, and who had perhaps overheard her there. Philostratus, too, seemed to remember the meeting; for his shrewd face—a pleasing mixture of grave and gay—lighted up at once with a subtle smile as he said:

"If I am not mistaken, I owe the same pleasure this evening to divine Caesar as to great Asklepios this morning?"

At this, Melissa cast a meaning glance at Coeranus and the lady, and, although surprise and alarm sealed her lips, her uplifted hands and whole gesture sufficiently expressed her entreaty that he would not betray her. He understood and obeyed. It pleased him to share a secret with this fair child. He had, in fact, overheard her, and understood with amazement that she was praying fervently for Caesar.

This stirred his curiosity to the highest pitch. So he said, in an undertone:

"All that I saw and heard in the temple is our secret, sweet maid. But what on earth can have prompted you to pray so urgently for Caesar? Has he done you or yours any great benefit?"

Melissa shook her head, and Philostratus went on with increased curiosity:

"Then are you one of those whose heart Eros can fire at the sight of an image, or the mere aspect of a man?"

To this she answered hastily:

"What an idea! No, no. Certainly not."

"No?" said her new friend, with greater surprise. "Then perhaps your hopeful young soul expects that, being still but a youth, he may, by the help of the gods, become, like Titus, a benefactor to the whole world?"

Melissa looked timidly at the matron, who was still talking with her brother-in-law, and hastily replied:

"They all call him a murderer! But I know for certain that he suffers fearful torments of mind and body; and one who knows many things told me that there was not one among all the millions whom Caesar governs who ever prays for him; and I was so sorry—I can not tell you—"

"And so," interrupted the philosopher, "you thought it praiseworthy and pleasing to the gods that you should be the first and only one to offer sacrifice for him, in secret, and of your own free will? That was how it came about? Well, child, you need not be ashamed of it."

But then suddenly his face clouded, and he asked, in a grave and altered voice:

"Are you a Christian?"

"No," she replied, firmly. "We are Greeks. How could I have offered a sacrifice of blood to Asklepios if I had believed in the crucified god?"

"Then," said Philostratus, and his eyes flashed brightly, "I may promise you, in the name of the gods, that your prayer and offering were pleasing in their eyes. I myself, noble girl, owe you a rare pleasure. But, tell me—how did you feel as you left the sanctuary?"

"Light-hearted, my lord, and content," she answered, with a frank, glad look in her fine eyes. "I could have sung as I went down the road, though there were people about."

"I should have liked to hear you," he said, kindly, and he still held her hand, which he had grasped with the amiable geniality that characterized him, when they were joined by the senator and his sister-in-law.

"Has she won your good offices?" asked Coeranus; and Philostratus replied, quickly, "Anything that it lies in my power to do for her shall certainly be done."

Berenike bade them both to join her in her own rooms, for everything that had to do with the banquet was odious to her; and as they went, Melissa told her new friend her brother's story. She ended it in the quiet sitting-room of the mistress of the house, an artistic but not splendid apartment, adorned only with the choicest works of early Alexandrian art. Philostratus listened attentively, but, before she could put her petition for help into words, he exclaimed:

"Then what we have to do is, to move Caesar to mercy, and that—Child, you know not what you ask!"

They were interrupted by a message from Seleukus, desiring Coeranus to join the other guests, and as soon as he had left them Berenike withdrew to take off the splendor she hated. She promised to return immediately and join their discussion, and Philostratus sat for a while lost in thought. Then he turned to Melissa and asked her:

"Would you for their sakes be able to make up your mind to face bitter humiliation, nay, perhaps imminent danger?"

"Anything! I would give my life for them!" replied the girl, with spirit, and her eyes gleamed with such enthusiastic self-sacrifice that his heart, though no longer young, warmed under their glow, and the principle to which he had sternly adhered since he had been near the imperial person, never to address a word to the sovereign but in reply, was blown to the winds.

Holding her hand in his, with a keen look into her eyes, he went on:

"And if you were required to do a thing from which many a man even would recoil—you would venture?"

And again the answer was a ready "Yes." Philostratus released her hand, and said:

"Then we will dare the worst. I will smooth the way for you, and to-morrow—do not start—tomorrow you yourself, under my protection, shall appeal to Caesar."

The color faded from the girl's cheeks, which had been flushed with fresh hopes, and her counselor had just expressed his wish to talk the matter over with the lady Berenike, when she came into the room. She was now dressed in mourning, and her pale, beautiful face showed the traces of the tears she had just shed. The dark shadows which, when they surround a woman's eyes, betray past storms of grief, as the halo round the moon —the eye of night— gives warning of storms to come, were deeper than ever; and when her sorrowful gaze fell on Melissa, the girl felt an almost irresistible longing to throw herself into her arms and weep on her motherly bosom.

Philostratus, too, was deeply touched by the appearance of this mother, who possessed so much, but for whom everything dearest to a woman's heart had been destroyed by a cruel stroke of Fate. He was glad to be able to tell her that he hoped to soften Caesar. Still, his plan was a bold one; Caracalla had been deeply offended by the scornful tone of the attacks on him, and Melissa's brother was perhaps the only one of the scoffers who had been taken. The crime of the Alexandrian wits could not be left unpunished. For such a desperate case only desperate remedies could avail; he therefore ventured to propose to conduct Melissa into Caesar's presence, that she might appeal to his clemency.

The matron started as though a scorpion had stung her. In great agitation, she threw her arm round the girl as if to shelter her from imminent danger, and Melissa, seeking help, laid her head on that kind breast. Berenike was reminded, by the scent that rose up from the girl's hair, of the hours when her own child had thus fondly clung to her. Her motherly heart had found a new object to love, and exclaiming, "Impossible!" she clasped Melissa more closely.

But Philostratus begged to be heard. Any plea urged by a third person he declared would only be the ruin of the rash mediator.

"Caracalla," he went on, looking at Melissa, "is terrible in his passions, no one can deny that; but of late severe suffering has made him irritably sensitive, and he insists on the strictest virtue in all who are about his person. He pays no heed to female beauty, and this sweet child, at any rate, will find many protectors. He shall know that the high-priest's wife, one of the best of women, keeps an anxious eye on Melissa's fate; and I myself, his mother's friend, shall be at hand. His passion for revenge, on the other hand, is boundless—no one living can control it; and not even the noble Julia can shield those who provoke it from a cruel end. If you do not know it, child, I can tell you that he had his brother Geta killed, though he took refuge in the arms of the mother who bore them both. You must understand the worst; and again I ask you, are you ready to risk all for those you love? Have you the courage to venture into the lion's den?"

Melissa clung more closely to the motherly woman, and her pale lips answered faintly but firmly, "I am ready, and he will grant my prayer."

"Child, child," cried Berenike in horror, "you know not what lies before you! You are dazzled by the happy confidence of inexperienced youth. I know what life is. I can see you, in your heart's blood, as red and pure as the blood of a lamb! I see—Ah, child! you do not know death and its terrible reality."

"I know it!" Melissa broke in with feverish excitement. "My dearest—my mother—I saw her die with these eyes. What did I not bury in her grave! And yet hope still lived in my heart; and though Caracalla may be a reckless murderer, he will do nothing to me, precisely because I am so feeble. And, lady, what am I? Of what account is my life if I lose my father, and my brothers, who are both on the high-road to greatness?"

"But you are betrothed," Berenike eagerly put in. "And your lover, you told me, is dear to you. What of him? He no doubt loves you, and, if you come to harm, sorrow will mar his young life."

At this Melissa clasped her hands over her face and sobbed aloud. "Show me, then, any other way—any! I will face the worst. But there is none; and if Diodoros were here he would not stop me; for what my heart prompts me to do is right, is my duty. But he is lying sick and with a clouded mind, and I can not ask him. O noble lady, kindness looks out of your eyes; cease to rub salt into my wounds! The task before me is hard enough already. But I would do it, and try to get speech with that terrible man, even if I had no one to protect me."

The lady had listened with varying feelings to this outpouring of the young girl's heart. Every instinct rebelled against the thought of sacrificing this pure, sweet creature to the fury of the tyrant whose wickedness was as unlimited as his power, and yet she saw no other chance of saving the artist, whom she held in affectionate regard. Her own noble heart understood the girl's resolve to purchase the life of those she loved, even with her blood; she, in the same place, would have done the same thing; and she thought to herself that it would have made her happy to see such a spirit in her own child. Her resistance melted away, and almost involuntarily she exclaimed, "Well, do what you feel to be right."

Melissa flew into her arms again with a grateful sense of release from a load, and Berenike did all she could to smooth the thorny way for her. She discussed every point with Philostratus as thoroughly as though for a child of her own; and, while the tumult came up from the banquet in the men's rooms, they settled that Berenike herself should conduct the girl to the wife of the high-priest of Serapis, the brother of Seleukus, and there await Melissa's return. Philostratus named the hour and other details, and then made further inquiries concerning the young artist whose mocking spirit had brought so much trouble on his family.

On this the lady led him into an adjoining room, where the portrait of her adored daughter was hanging. It was surrounded by a thick wreath of violets, the dead girl's favorite flower. The beautiful picture was lighted up by two three-branched lamps on high stands; and Philostratus, a connoisseur who had described many paintings with great taste and vividness, gazed in absorbed silence at the lovely features, which were represented with rare mastery and the inspired devotion of loving admiration. At last he turned to the mother, exclaiming:

"Happy artist, to have such a subject! It is a work worthy of the early, best period, and of a master of the time of Apelies. The daughter who has been snatched from you, noble lady, was indeed matchless, and no sorrow is too deep to do her justice. But the divinity who has taken her knows also how to give; and this portrait has preserved for you a part of what you loved. This picture, too, may influence Melissa's fate; for Caesar has a fine taste in art, and one of the wants of our time which has helped to embitter him is the paralyzed state of the imitative arts. It will be easier to win his favor for the painter who did this portrait than for a man of noble birth. He needs such painters as this Alexander for the Pinakothek in the splendid baths he has built at Rome. If you would but lend me this treasure to-morrow—"

But she interrupted him with a decisive "Never!" and laid her hand on the frame as if to protect it. Philostratus, however, was not to be put off; he went on in a tone of the deepest disappointment: "This portrait is yours, and no one can wonder at your refusal. We must, therefore, consider how to attain our end without this important ally." Berenike's gaze had lingered calmly on the sweet face while he spoke, looking more and more deeply into the beautiful, expressive features. All was silent.

At last she slowly turned to Melissa, who stood gazing sadly at the ground, and said in a low voice: "She resembled you in many ways. The gods had formed her to shed joy and light around her. Where she could wipe away a tear she always did so. Her portrait is speechless, and yet it tells me to act as she herself would have acted. If this work can indeed move Caracalla to clemency, then—You, Philostratus, really think so?"

"Yes," he replied, decisively. "There can be no better mediator for Alexander than this work." Berenike drew herself up, and said:

"Well, then, to-morrow morning early, I will send it to you at the Serapeum. The portrait of the dead may perish if it may but save the life of him who wrought it so lovingly." She turned away her face as she gave the philosopher her hand, and then hastily left the room.

Melissa flew after her and, with overflowing gratitude, besought the sobbing lady not to weep.

"I know something that will bring you greater comfort than my brother's picture: I mean the living image of your Korinna—a young girl; she is here in Alexandria."

"Zeno's daughter Agatha?" said Berenike; and when Melissa said yes, it was she, the lady went on with a deep sigh: "Thanks for your kind thought, my child; but she, too, is lost to me."

And as she spoke she sank on a couch, saying, in a low voice, "I would rather be alone."

Melissa modestly withdrew into the adjoining room, and Philostratus, who had been lost in the contemplation of the picture, took his leave.

He did not make use of the imperial chariot in waiting for him, but returned to his lodgings on foot, in such good spirits, and so well satisfied with himself, as he had not been before since leaving Rome.

When Berenike had rested in solitude for some little time she recalled Melissa, and took as much care of her young guest as though she were her lost darling, restored to her after a brief absence. First she allowed the girl to send for Argutis; and when she had assured the faithful slave that all promised well, she dismissed him with instructions to await at home his young mistress's orders, for that Melissa would for the present find shelter under her roof.

When the Gaul had departed, she desired her waiting-woman, Johanna, to fetch her brother. During her absence the lady explained to Melissa that they both were Christians. They were freeborn, the children of a freedman of Berenike's house. Johannes had at an early age shown so much intelligence that they had acceded to his wish to be educated as a lawyer. He was now one of the most successful pleaders in the city; but he always used his eloquence, which he had perfected not only at Alexandria but also at Carthage, by preference in the service of accused Christians. In his leisure hours he would visit the condemned in prison, speak comfort to them, and give them presents out of the fine profits he derived from his business among the wealthy. He was the very man to go and see her father and brothers; he would revive their spirits, and carry them her greeting.

When, presently, the Christian arrived he expressed himself as very ready to undertake this commission. His sister was already busied in packing wine and other comforts for the captives-more, no doubt, as Johannes told Berenike, than the three men could possibly consume, even if their imprisonment should be a long one. His smile showed how confidently he counted on the lady's liberality, and Melissa quickly put her faith in the young Christian, who would have reminded her of her brother Philip, but that his slight figure was more upright, and his long hair quite smooth, without a wave or curl. His eyes, above all, were unlike Philip's; for they looked out on the world with a gaze as mild as Philip's were keen and inquiring.

Melissa gave him many messages for her father and brothers, and when the lady Berenike begged him to take care that the portrait of her daughter was safely carried to the Serapeum, where it was to contribute to mollify Caesar in the painter's favor, he praised her determination, and modestly added: "For how long may we call our own any of these perishable joys? A day, perhaps a year, at most a lustrum. But eternity is long, and those who, for its sake, forget time and set all their hopes on eternity —which is indeed time to the soul—soon cease to bewail the loss of any transitory treasure, were it the noblest and dearest. Oh, would that I could lead you to place your hopes on eternity, best of women and most true-hearted mother! Eternity, which not the wisest brain can conceive of!—I tell you, lady, for you are a philosopher—that is the hardest and therefore the grandest idea for human thought to compass. Fix your eye on that, and in its infinite realm, which must be your future home, you will meet her again whom you have lost— not her image returned to you, but herself."

"Cease," interrupted the matron, with impatient sharpness. "I know what you are aiming at. But to conceive of eternity is the prerogative of the immortals; our intellect is wrecked in the attempt. Our wings melt like those of Ikarus, and we fall into the ocean—the ocean of madness, to which I have often been near enough. You Christians fancy you know all about eternity, and if you are right in that—But I will not reopen that old discussion. Give me back my child for a year, a month, a day even, as she was before murderous disease laid hands on her, and I will make you a free gift of your cuckoo-cloud-land of eternity, and of the remainder of my own life on earth into the bargain."

The vehement woman trembled with renewed sorrow, as if shivering with ague; but as soon as she had recovered her self-command enough to speak calmly, she exclaimed to the lawyer:

"I do not really wish to vex you, Johannes. I esteem you, and you are dear to me. But if you wish our friendship to continue, give up these foolish attempts to teach tortoises to fly. Do all you can for the poor prisoners; and if you—"

"By daybreak to-morrow I will be with them," Johannes said, and he hastily took leave.

As soon as they were alone Berenike observed "There he goes, quite offended, as if I had done him a wrong. That is the way with all these Christians. They think it their duty to force on others what they themselves think right, and any one who turns a deaf ear to their questionable truths they at once set down as narrow-minded, or as hostile to what is good. Agatha, of whom you were just now speaking, and Zeno her father, my husband's brother, are Christians. I had hoped that Korinna's death would have brought the child back to us; I have longed to see her, and have heard much that is sweet about her: but a common sorrow, which so often brings divided hearts together, has only widened the gulf between my husband and his brother. The fault is not on our side. Nay, I was rejoiced when, a few hours after the worst was over, a letter from Zeno informed me that he and his daughter would come to see us the same evening. But the letter itself"—and her voice began to quiver with indignation—"compelled us to beg him not to come. It is scarcely credible—and I should do better not to pour fresh oil on my wrath—but he bade us 'rejoice'; three, four, five times he repeated the cruel words. And he wrote in a pompous strain of the bliss and rapture which awaited our lost child—and this to a mother whose heart had been utterly broken but a few hours before by a fearful stroke of Fate! He would meet the bereaved, grieving, lonely mourner with a smile on his lips! Rejoice! This climax of cruelty or aberration has parted us forever. Why, our black gardener, whose god is a tree-stump that bears only the faintest likeness to humanity, melted into tears at the news; and Zeno, our brother, the uncle of that broken dower, could be glad and bid us rejoice! My husband thinks that hatred and the long-standing feud prompted his pen. For my part, I believe it was only this Christian frenzy which made him suggest that I should sink lower than the brutes, who defend their young with their lives. Seleukus has long since forgiven him for his conduct in withdrawing his share of the capital from the business when he became a Christian, to squander it on the baser sort; but this 'Rejoice' neither he nor I can forgive, though things which pierce me to the heart often slide off him like water off grease."

Her black hair had come down as she delivered this vehement speech, and, when she ceased, her flushed cheeks and the fiery glow of her eyes gave the majestic woman in her dark robes an aspect which terrified Melissa.

She, too, thought this "Rejoice," under such circumstances, unseemly and insulting; but she kept her opinion to herself, partly out of modesty and partly because she did not wish to encourage the estrangement between this unhappy lady and the niece whose mere presence would have been so great a comfort to her.

When Johanna returned to lead her to a bedroom, she gave a sigh of relief; but the lady expressed a wish to keep Melissa near her, and in a low voice desired the waiting-woman to prepare a bed for her in the adjoining room, by the side of Korinna's, which was never to be disturbed. Then, still greatly excited, she invited Melissa into her daughter's pretty room.

There she showed her everything that Korinna had especially cared for. Her bird hung in the same place; her lap-dog was sleeping in a basket, on the cushion which Berenike had embroidered for her child. Melissa had to admire the dead girl's lute, and her first piece of weaving, and the elegant loom of ebony and ivory in which she had woven it. And Berenike repeated to the girl the verses which Korinna had composed, in imitation of Catullus, on the death of a favorite bird. And although Melissa's eyes were almost closing with fatigue, she forced herself to attend to it all, for she saw now how much her sympathy pleased her kind friend.

Meanwhile the voices of the men, who had done eating and were now drinking, came louder and louder into the women's apartments. When the merriment of her guests rose to a higher pitch than usual, or something amusing gave rise to a shout of laughter, Berenike shrank, and either muttered some unintelligible threat or besought the forgiveness of her daughter's manes.

It seemed to be a relief to her to rush from one mood to the other; but neither in her grief, nor when her motherly feeling led her to talk, nor yet in her wrath, did she lose her perfect dignity. All Melissa saw and heard moved her to pity or to horror. And meanwhile she was worn out with anxiety for her family, and with increasing fatigue.

At last, however, she was released. A gay chorus of women's voices and flutes came up from the banqueting-hall. With a haughty mien and dilated nostrils Berenike listened to the first few bars. That such a song should be heard in her house of woe was too much; with her own hand she closed the shutters over the window next her; then she bade her young guest go to bed.

Oh, how glad was the overtired girl to stretch herself on the soft couch! As usual, before going to sleep, she told her mother in the spirit all the history of the day. Then she prayed to the manes of the departed to lend her aid in the heavy task before her; but in the midst of her prayer sleep overcame her, and her young bosom was already rising and falling in regular breathing when she was roused by a visit from the lady Berenike.

Melissa suddenly beheld her at the head of the bed, in a flowing white night-dress, with her hair unpinned, and holding a silver lamp in her hand; and the girl involuntarily put up her arms as if to protect herself, for she fancied that the daemon of madness stared out of those large black eyes. But the unhappy woman's expression changed, and she looked down kindly on Melissa. She quietly set the lamp on the table, and then, as the cool nightbreeze blew in through the open window, to which there was no shutter, she tenderly wrapped the white woolen blanket round Melissa, and muttered to herself, "She liked it so."

Then she knelt down by the side of the bed, pressed her lips on the brow of the girl, now fully awake, and said:

"And you, too, are fair to look upon. He will grant your prayer!"

Then she asked Melissa about her lover, her father, her mother, and at last she, unexpectedly, asked her in a whisper:

"Your brother Alexander, the painter—My daughter, though in death, inspired his soul with love. Yes, Korinna was dear to him. Her image is living in his soul. Am I right? Tell me the truth!"

On this Melissa confessed how deeply the painter had been impressed by the dead girl's beauty, and that he had given her his heart and soul with a fervor of devotion of which she had never imagined him capable. And the poor mother smiled as she heard it, and murmured, "I was sure of it."

But then she shook her head, sadly, and said "Fool that I am!"

At last she bade Melissa good-night, and went back to her own bedroom. There Johanna was awaiting her, and while she was plaiting her mistress's hair the matron said, threateningly:

"If the wretch should not spare even her"—She was interrupted by loud shouts of mirth from the banqueting-hall, and among the laughing voices she fancied that she recognized her husband's. She started up with a vehement movement, and exclaimed, in angry excitement:

"Seleukus might have prevented such an outrage! Oh, I know that sorrowing father's heart! Fear, vanity, ambition, love of pleasure—"

"But consider," Johanna broke in, "to cross Caesar's wish is to forfeit life!"

"Then he should have died!" replied the matron, with stern decision.

CHAPTER XVI.

Before sunrise the wind changed. Heavy clouds bore down from the north, darkening the clear sky of Alexandria. By the time the market was filling it was raining in torrents, and a cold breeze blew over the town from the lake. Philostratus had only allowed himself a short time for sleep, sitting till long after midnight over his history of Apolonius of Tyana. His aim was to prove, by the example of this man, that a character not less worthy of imitation than that of the lord of the Christians might be formed in the faith of the ancients, and nourished by doctrines produced by the many-branched tree of Greek religion and philosophy. Julia Domna, Caracalla's mother, had encouraged the philosopher in this task, which was to show her passionate and criminal son the dignity of moderation and virtue. The book was also to bring home to Caesar the religion of his forefathers and his country in all its beauty and elevating power; for hitherto he had vacillated from one form to another, had not even rejected Christianity, with which his nurse had tried to inoculate him as a child, and had devoted himself to every superstition of his time in a way which had disgusted those about him. It had been particularly interesting to the writer, with a view to the purpose of this work, to meet with a girl who practiced all the virtues the Christians most highly prized, without belonging to that sect, who were always boasting of the constraining power of their religion in conducing to pure morality.

In his work the day before he had taken occasion to regret the small recognition his hero had met with among those nearest to him. In this, as in other respects, he seemed to have shared the fate of Jesus Christ, whose name, however, Philostratus purposely avoided mentioning. Now, to-night, he reflected on the sacrifice offered by Melissa for Caesar whom she knew not, and he wrote the following words as though proceeding from the pen of Apollonius himself: "I know well how good a thing it is to regard all the world as my home, and all mankind as my brethren and friends; for we are all of the same divine race, and have all one Father."

Then, looking up from the papyrus, he murmured to himself: "From such a point of view as this Melissa might see in Caracalla a friend and a brother. If only now it were possible to rouse the conscience of that imperial criminal!"

He took up the written sheet on which he had begun a dissertation as to what conscience is, as exerting a choice between good and evil. He had written: "Understanding governs what we purpose; consciousness governs what our understanding resolves upon. Hence, if our understanding choose the good, consciousness is satisfied."

How flat it sounded! It could have no effect in that form.

Melissa had confessed with far greater warmth what her feelings had been after she had sacrificed for the suffering sinner. Every one, no doubt, would feel the same who, when called on to choose between good and evil, should prefer the good; so he altered and expanded the last words: "Thus consciousness sends a man with song and gladness into the sanctuaries and groves, into the roads, and wherever mortals live. Even in sleep the song makes itself heard, and a happy choir from the land of dreams lift up their voices about his bed."

That was better! This pleasing picture might perhaps leave some impression on the soul of the young criminal, in whom a preference for good could still, though rarely, be fanned to a flame. Caesar read what Philostratus wrote, because he took pleasure in the form of his work; and this sentence would not have been written in vain if only it should prompt Caracalla in some cases, however few, to choose the good.

The philosopher was fully determined to do his utmost for Melissa and her brothers. He had often brought pictures under Caesar's notice, for he was the first living authority as a connoisseur of painting, and as having written many descriptions of pictures. He built some hopes, too, on Melissa's innocence; and so the worthy man, when he retired to rest, looked forward with confidence to the work of mediation, which was by no means devoid of danger.

But next morning it presented itself in a less promising light. The clouded sky, the storm, and rain might have a fatal effect on Caesar's temper; and when he heard that old Galen, after examining his patient and prescribing certain remedies, had yesterday evening taken ship, leaving Caracalla in a frenzy of rage which had culminated in slight convulsions, he almost repented of his promise. However, he felt himself pledged; so as early as possible he went to Caesar's rooms, prepared for the worst.

His gloomy anticipations were aggravated by the scene which met his eyes.

In the anteroom he found the chief men of the city and some representative members of the Alexandrian Senate, who were anxious for an audience of their imperial visitor. They had been commanded to attend at an unusually early hour, and had already been kept a long time waiting.

When Philostratus—who was always free to enter Caesar's presence—made his appearance, Caracalla was seating himself on the throne which had been placed for him in the splendidly fitted audience-chamber. He had come from his bath, and was wrapped in the comfortable white woolen robe which he wore on leaving it. His "friends" as they were called, senators, and other men of mark, stood round in considerable numbers, among them the high-priest of Serapis. Pandion, Caesar's charioteer, was occupied, under the sovereign's instructions, in fastening the lion's chain to the ring fixed for the purpose in the floor by the side of the throne; and as the beast, whose collar had been drawn too tight, uttered a low, complaining growl, Caracalla scolded the favorite. As soon as he caught sight of Philostratus, he signed to him to approach:

"Do you see nothing strange in me?" he whispered. "Your Phoebus Apollo appeared to me in a dream. He laid his hand on my shoulder toward morning; indeed, I saw only horrible faces." Then he pointed out of the window, exclaiming:

"The god hides his face to-day. Gloomy days have often brought me good fortune; but this is a strange experience of the eternal sunshine of Egypt! Men and sky have given me the same kind welcome; gray, gray, and always gray—without and within—and my poor soldiers out on the square! Macrinus tells me they are complaining. But my father's advice was sound: "Keep them content, and never mind anything else." The heads of the town are waiting outside; they must give up their palaces to the bodyguard; if they murmur, let them try for themselves how they like sleeping on the soaking ground under dripping tents. It may cool their hot blood, and perhaps dilute the salt of their wit.—Show them in, Theocritus."

He signed to the actor, and when he humbly asked whether Caesar had forgotten to exchange his morning wrapper for another dress, Caracalla laughed contemptuously, and replied:

"Why, an empty corn-sack over my shoulders would be dress enough for this rabble of traders!" He stretched his small but muscular frame out at full length, resting his head on his hand, and his comely face, which had lost the suffering look it had worn the day before, suddenly changed in expression. As was his habit when he wished to inspire awe or fear, he knit his brows in deep furrows, set his teeth tightly, and assumed a suspicious and sinister scowl.

The deputation entered, bowing low, headed by the exegetes, the head of the city, and Timotheus, the chief-priest of Serapis. After these came the civic authorities, the members of the senate, and then, as representing the large Jewish colony in the city, their alabarch or head- man. It was easy to see in each one as he came in, that the presence of the lion, who had raised his head at their approach, was far from encouraging; and a faint, scornful smile parted Caracalla's lips as he noted the cowering knees of these gorgeously habited courtiers. The high-priest alone, who, as Caesar's host, had gone up to the side of the throne, and two or three others, among them the governor of the town, a tall, elderly man of Macedonian descent, paid no heed to the brute. The Macedonian bowed to his sovereign with calm dignity, and in the name of the municipally hoped he had rested well. He then informed Caesar what shows and performances were prepared in his honor, and finally named the considerable sum which had been voted by the town of Alexandria to express to him their joy at his visit. Caracalla waved his hand, and said, carelessly:

"The priest of Alexander, as idiologos, will receive the gold with the temple tribute. We can find use for it. We knew that you were rich. But what do you want for your money? What have you to ask?"

"Nothing, noble Caesar," replied the governor. "Thy gracious presence—"

Caracalla interrupted him with a long-drawn "Indeed!" Then, leaning forward, he gave him a keen, oblique look. "No one but the gods has nothing to wish for; so it must be that you are afraid to ask. What can that avail, unless to teach me that you look for nothing but evil from me; that you are suspicious of me? And if that is so, you fear me; and if you fear, you hate me. The insults I have received in this house sufficiently prove the fact. And if you hate me," and he sprang up and shook his fist, "I must protect myself!"

"Great Caesar," the exegetes began, in humble deprecation, but Caracalla went on, wrathfully:

"I know when I have to protect myself, and from whom. It is not well to trifle with me! An insolent tongue is easily hidden behind the lips; but heads are less easy to hide, and I shall be content with them. Tell that to your Alexandrian wits! Macrinus will inform you of all else. You may go."

During this speech the lion, excited by his master's furious gestures, had risen on his feet and showed his terrible teeth to the delegates. At this their courage sank. Some laid their hands on their bent knees, as if to shield them; others had gradually sidled to the door before Caesar had uttered the last word. Then, in spite of the efforts of the governor and the alabarch to detain them, in the hope of pacifying the potentate, as soon as they heard the word "go," they hurried out; and, for better or for worse, the few bolder spirits had to follow.

As soon as the door was closed upon them, Caesar's features lost their cruel look. He patted the lion with soothing words of praise, and exclaimed, contemptuously:

"These are the descendants of the Macedonians, with whom the greatest of heroes conquered the world! Who was that fat old fellow who shrank into himself so miserably, and made for the door while I was yet speaking?"

"Kimon, the chief of the night-watch and guardian of the peace of the city," replied the high-priest of Alexander, who as a Roman had kept his place by the throne; and Theocritus put in:

"The people must sleep badly under the ward of such a coward. Let him follow the prefect, noble Caesar."

"Send him his dismissal at once," said Caracalla; "but see that his successor is a man."

He then turned to the high-priest, and politely requested him to assist Theocritus in choosing a new head for the town-guard, and Timotheus and the favorite quitted the room together.

Philostratus took ingenious advantage of the incident, by at once informing the emperor that it had come to his knowledge that this coward, so worthily dismissed from office, had, on the merest suspicion, cast into prison a painter who was undoubtedly one of the first of living artists, and with him his guiltless relations.

"I will not have it!" Caesar broke out. "Nothing but blood will do any good here, and petty aggravations will only stir their bile and increase their insolence. Is the painter of whom you speak an Alexandrian?—I pine for the open air, but the wind blows the rain against the windows."

"In the field," the philosopher remarked, "you have faced the weather heroically enough. Here, in the city, enjoy what is placed before you. Only yesterday I still believed that the art of Apelles was utterly degenerate. But since then I have changed my opinion, for I have seen a portrait which would be an ornament to the Pinakothek in your baths. The northern windows are closed, or, in this land of inundations, and in such weather as this, we might find ourselves afloat even under cover of a roof; so it is too dark here to judge of a painting, but your dressing-room is more favorably situated, and the large window there will serve our purpose. May I be allowed the pleasure of showing you there the work of the imprisoned artist?"

Caesar nodded, and led the way, accompanied by his lion and followed by the philosopher, who desired an attendant to bring in the picture.

In this room it was much lighter than in the audience-chamber, and while Caracalla awaited, with Philostratus, the arrival of the painting, his Indian body-slave, a gift from the Parthian king, silently and skillfully dressed his thin hair. The sovereign sighed deeply, and pressed his hand to his brow as though in pain. The philosopher ventured to approach him, and there was warm sympathy in his tone as he asked:

"What ails you, Bassianus? Just now you bore all the appearance of a healthy, nay, and of a terrible man!"

"It is better again already," replied the sovereign." And yet—!"

He groaned again, and then confessed that only yesterday he had in the same way been tortured with pain.

"The attack came on in the morning, as you know," he went on, "and when it was past I went down into the court of sacrifice; my feet would scarcely carry me. Curiosity—and they were waiting for me; and some great sign might be shown! Besides, some excitement helps me through this torment. But there was nothing—nothing! Heart, lungs, liver, all in their right place.— And then, Galenus—What I like is bad for me, what I loathe is wholesome. And again and again the same foolish question, 'Do you wish to escape an early death?' And all with an air as though Death were a slave at his command—He can, no doubt, do more than others, and has preserved his own life I know not how long. Well, and it is his duty to prolong mine.

"I am Caesar. I had a right to insist on his remaining here. I did so; for he knows my malady, and describes it as if he felt it himself. I ordered him— nay, I entreated him. But he adhered to his own way. He went—he is gone!"

"But he may be of use to you, even at a distance," Philostratus said.

"Did he do anything for my father, or for me in Rome, where he saw me every day?" retorted Caesar. "He can mitigate and relieve the suffering, but that is all; and of all the others, is there one fit to hand him a cup of water? Perhaps he would be willing to cure me, but he can not; for I tell you, Philostratus, the gods will not have it so. You know what sacrifices I have offered, what gifts I have brought. I have prayed, I have abased myself before them, but none will hear. One or another of the gods, indeed, appears to me not infrequently as Apollo did last night. But is it because he favors me? First, he laid his hand on my shoulder, as my father used to do; but his was so heavy, that the weight pressed me down till I fell on my knees, crushed. This is no good sign, you think? I see it in your face. I do not myself think so. And how loudly I have called on him, of all the gods! The whole empire, they say, men and women alike, besought the immortals unbidden for the welfare of Titus. I, too, am their lord; but"—and he laughed bitterly—"who has ever raised a hand in prayer for me of his own impulse? My own mother always named my brother first. He has paid for it,—But the rest!"

"They fear rather than love you," replied the philosopher. "He to whom Phoebus Apollo appears may always expect some good to follow. And yesterday—a happy omen, too—I overheard by chance a young Greek girl, who believed herself unobserved, who of her own prompting fervently entreated Asklepios to heal you. Nay, she collected all the coins in her little purse, and had a goat and a cock sacrificed in your behalf."

"And you expect me to believe that!" said Caracalla, with a scornful laugh.

But Philostratus eagerly replied:

"It is the pure truth. I went to the little temple because it was said that Apollonius had left some documents there. Every word from his pen is, as you know, of value to me in writing his history. The little library was screened off from the cella by a curtain, and while I was hunting through the manuscripts I heard a woman's voice."

"It spoke for some other Bassianus, Antoninus, Tarautus, or whatever they choose to call me," Caesar broke in.

"Nay, my lord, not so. She prayed for you, the son of Severus. I spoke to her afterwards. She had seen you yesterday morning, and fancied she had noted how great and severe your sufferings were. This had gone to her heart. So she went thither to pray and sacrifice for you, although she knew that you were prosecuting her brother, the very painter of whom I spoke. I would you too could have heard how fervently she addressed the god, and then Hygeia!"

"A Greek, you say?" Caracalla remarked. "And she really did not know you, or dream that you could hear her?"

"No, my lord; assuredly not. She is a sweet maid, and if you would care to see her—"

Caesar had listened to the tale with great attention and evident expectancy; but suddenly his face clouded, and, heedless of the slaves who, under the guidance of his chamberlain Adventus, had now brought in the portrait, he sprang up, went close to Philostratus, and stormed out:

"Woe to you if you lie to me! You want to get the brother out of prison, and then, by chance, you come across the sister who is praying for me! A fable to cheat a child with!"

"I am speaking the truth," replied Philostratus, coolly, though the rapid winking of Caesar's eyelids warned him that his blood was boiling with wrath.

"It was from the sister, whom I overheard in the temple, that I learned of her brother's peril, and I afterward saw that portrait."

Caracalla stared at the floor for a moment in silence; then he looked up, and said, in a tone husky with agitation:

"I only long for anything which may bring me nearer to the perverse race over whom I rule, be it what it may. You offer it me. You are the only man who never asked me for anything. I have believed you to be as righteous as all other men are not. And now if you, if this time—"

He lowered his tones, which had become somewhat threatening, and went on very earnestly: "By all you hold most sacred on earth, I ask you, Did the girl pray for me, and of her own free impulse, not knowing that any one could hear her?"

"I swear it, by the head of my mother!" replied Philostratus, solemnly.

"Your mother?" echoed Caesar, and his brow began to clear. But suddenly the gleam of satisfaction, which for a moment had embellished his features, vanished, and with a sharp laugh he added: "And my mother! Do you suppose that I do not know what she requires of you? It is solely to please her that you, a free man, remain with me. For her sake you are bold enough to try now and then to quell the stormy sea of my passions. You do it with a grace, so I submit. And now my hand is raised to strike a wretch who mocks at me; he is a painter, of some talent, so, of course, you take him under your protection. Then, in a moment, your inventive genius devises a praying sister. Well, there is in that something which might indeed mollify me. But you would betray Bassianus ten times over to save an artist. And then, how my mother would fly to show her gratitude to the man who could quell her furious son! Your mother!— But I only squint when it suits me. My eye must become dimmer than it yet is before I fail to see the connection of ideas which led you to swear by your mother. You were thinking of mine when you spoke. To please her, you would deceive her son. But as soon as he touches the lie it vanishes into thin air, for it has no more substance than a soap bubble!" The last words were at once sad, angry, and scornful; but the philosopher, who had listened at first with astonishment and then with indignation, could no longer contain himself.

"Enough!" he cried to the angry potentate, in an imperious tone. Then, drawing himself up, he went on with offended dignity:

"I know what the end has been of so many who have aroused your wrath, and yet I have courage enough to tell you to your face, that to injustice, the outcome of distrust, you add the most senseless insult. Or do you really think that a just man—for so you have called me more than once— would outrage the manes of the beloved woman who bore him to please the mother of another man, even though she be Caesar's? What I swear to by the head of my mother, friend and foe alike must believe; and he who does not, must hold me to be the vilest wretch on earth; my presence can only be an offense to him. So I beg you to allow me to return to Rome."

The words were manly and spoken firmly, and they pleased Caracalla; for the joy of believing in the philosopher's statement outweighed every other feeling. And since he regarded Philostratus as the incarnation of goodness— though he had lost faith in that—his threat of leaving disturbed him greatly. He laid his hand on his brave adviser's arm, and assured him that he was only too happy to believe a thing so incredible.

Any witness of the scene would have supposed this ruthless fatricide, this tyrant—whose intercourse with the visions of a crazed and unbridled fancy made him capable of any folly, and who loved to assume the aspect of a cruel misanthrope—to be a docile disciple, who cared for nothing but to recover the favor and forgiveness of his master. And Philostratus, knowing this man, and the human heart, did not make it too easy for him to achieve his end. When he at last gave up his purpose of returning to Rome, and had more fully explained to Caesar how and where he had met Melissa, and what he had heard about her brother the painter, he lifted the wrapper from Korinna's portrait, placed it in a good light, and pointed out to Caracalla the particular beauties of the purely Greek features.

It was with sincere enthusiasm that he expatiated on the skill with which the artist had reproduced in color the noble lines which Caracalla so much admired in the sculpture of the great Greek masters; how warm and tender the flesh was; how radiant the light of those glorious eyes; how living the waving hair, as though it still breathed of the scented oil! And when Philostratus explained that though Alexander had no doubt spoken some rash and treasonable words, he could not in any case be the author of the insulting verses which had been found at the Serapeum with the rope, Caracalla echoed his praises of the picture, and desired to see both the painter and his sister.

That morning, as he rose from his bed, he had been informed that the planets which had been seen during the past night from the observatory of the Serapeum, promised him fortune and happiness in the immediate future. He was himself a practiced star-reader, and the chief astrologer of the temple had pointed out to him how peculiarly favorable the constellation was whence he had deduced his prediction. Then, Phoebus Apollo had appeared to him in a dream; the auguries from the morning's sacrifices had all been favorable; and, before he dispatched Philostratus to fetch Melissa, he added:

"It is strange! The best fortune has always come to me from a gloomy sky. How brightly the sun shone on my marriage with the odious Plautilla! It has rained, on the contrary, on almost all my victories; and it was under a heavy storm that the oracle assured me the soul of Alexander the Great had selected this tortured frame in which to live out his too early ended years on earth. Can such coincidence be mere chance? Phoebus Apollo, your favorite divinity—and that, too, of the sage of Tyana—may perhaps have been angry with me. He who purified himself from blood-guiltiness after killing the Python is the god of expiation. I will address myself to him, like the noble hero of your book. This morning the god visited me again; so I will have such sacrifice slain before him as never yet was offered. Will that satisfy you, O philosopher hard to be appeased?"

"More than satisfy me, my Bassianus," replied Philostratus. "Yet remember that, according to Apollonius, the sacrifice is effective only through the spirit in which it is offered."

"Always a 'but' and an 'if'!" exclaimed Caracalla, as his friend left the room to call Melissa from the high-priest's quarters, where she was waiting.

For the first time for some days Caesar found himself alone. Leading the lion by the collar, he went to the window. The rain had ceased, but black clouds still covered the heavens. Below him lay the opening of the street of Hermes into the great square, swarming with human life, and covered with the now drenched tents of the soldiery; and his eyes fell on that of a centurion, a native of Alexandria, just then receiving a visit from his family, to whom the varied fortunes of a warrior's life had brought him back once more.

The bearded hero held an infant in his arms—assuredly his own—while a girl and boy clung to him, gazing up in his face with wondering black eyes; and another child, of about three, paying no heed to the others, was crowing as it splashed through a puddle with its little bare feet. Two women, one young and one elderly, the man's mother and his wife, no doubt, seemed to hang on his lips as he recounted perhaps some deed of valor.

The tuba sounded to arms. He kissed the infant, and carefully laid it on its mother's bosom; then he took up the boy and the girl, laughingly caught the little one, and pressed his bearded lips to each rosy mouth in turn. Last of all he clasped the young wife to his breast, gently stroked her hair, and whispered something in her ear at which she smiled up at him through her tears and then blushingly looked down. His mother patted him fondly on the shoulder, and, as they parted, he kissed her too on her wrinkled brow.

Caracalla had remarked this centurion once before; his name was Martialis, and he was a simple, commonplace, but well-conducted creature, who had often distinguished himself by his contempt for death. The imperial visit to Alexandria had meant for him a return home and the greatest joy in life. How many arms had opened to receive the common soldier; how many hearts had beat high at his coming! Not a day, it was certain, had passed since his arrival without prayers going up to Heaven for his preservation, from his mother, his wife, and his children. And he, the ruler of the world, had thought it impossible that one, even one of his millions of subjects, should have prayed for him. Who awaited him with a longing heart? Where was his home?

He had first seen the light in Gaul. His father was an African; his mother was born in Syria. The palace at Rome, his residence, he did not care to remember. He traveled about the empire, leaving as wide a space as possible between himself and that house of doom, from which he could never wipe out the stain of his brother's blood.

And his mother? She feared—perhaps she hated him—her first-born son, since he had killed her younger darling. What did she care for him, so long as she had her philosophers to argue with, who knew how to ply her with delicate flattery?

Then Plautilla, his wife? His father had compelled him to marry her, the richest heiress in the world, whose dowry had been larger than the collected treasure of a dozen queens; and as he thought of the sharp features of that insignificant, sour-faced, and unspeakably pretentious creature, he shuddered with aversion.

He had banished her, and then had her murdered. Others had done the deed, and it did not strike him that he was responsible for the crime committed in his service; but her loveless heart, without a care for him—her bird-sharp face, looking out like a well-made mask from her abundant hair—and her red, pinched lips, were very present to him. What cutting words those lips could speak; what senseless demands they had uttered; and nothing more insolent could be imagined than her way of pursing them up if at any time he had suggested a kiss!

His child? One had been born to him, but it had followed its mother into exile and to the grave. The little thing, which he had scarcely known, was so inseparable from its detested mother that he had mourned it no more than her. It was well that the assassins, without any orders from him, should have cut short that wretched life. He could not long for the embraces of the monster which should have united Plautilla's vices and his own.

Among the men about his person, there was not one for whom other hearts beat warmer; no creature that loved him excepting his lion; no spot on earth where he was looked for with gladness. He waited, as for some marvel, to see the one human being who had spontaneously entreated the gods for him. The girl must probably be a poor, tearful creature, as weak of brain as she was soft-hearted.

There stood the centurion at the head of his maniple, and raised his staff. Enviable man! How content he looked; how clearly he spoke the word of command! And how healthy the vulgar creature must be—while he, Caesar, was suffering that acute headache again! He gnashed his teeth, and felt a strong impulse to spoil the happiness of that shameless upstart. If he were sent packing to Spain, now, or to Pontus, there would be an end of his gladness. The centurion should know what it was to be a solitary soul.

Acting on this malignant impulse, he had raised his hand to his mouth to shout the cruel order to a tribune, when suddenly the clouds parted, and the glorious sun of Africa appeared in a blue island amid the ocean of gray, cheering the earth with glowing sheaves of rays. The beams were blinding as they came reflected from the armor and weapons of the men, reminding Caesar of the god to whom he had just vowed an unparalleled sacrifice.

Philostratus had often praised Phoebus Apollo above all gods, because wherever he appeared there was light, irradiating not the earth alone but men's souls; and because, as the lord of music and harmony, he aided men to arrive at that morally pure and equable frame of mind which was accordant and pleasing to his glorious nature. Apollo had conquered the dark heralds of the storm, and Caracalla looked up. Before this radiant witness he was ashamed to carry out his dark purpose, and he said, addressing the sun:

"For thy sake, Phoebus Apollo, I spare the man." Then, pleased with himself, he looked down again. The restraint he had laid upon himself struck him as in fact a great and noble effort, accustomed as he was to yield to every impulse. But at the same time he observed that the clouds, which had so often brought him good fortune, were dispersing, and this gave him fresh uneasiness. Dazzled by the flood of sunshine which poured in at the window, he withdrew discontentedly into the room. If this bright day were to bring disaster? If the god disdained his offering?

But was not Apollo, perhaps, like the rest of the immortals, an idol of the fancy, living only in the imagination of men who had devised it? Stern thinkers and pious folks, like the skeptics and the Christians, laughed the whole tribe of the Olympians to scorn. Still, the hand of Phoebus Apollo had rested heavily on his shoulders in his dream. His power, after all, might be great. The god must have the promised sacrifice, come what might. Bitter wrath rose up in his soul at this thought, as it had often done before, with the immortals, against whom he, the all-powerful, was impotent. If only for an hour they could be his subjects, he would make them rue the sufferings by which they spoiled his existence.

"He is called Martialis. I will remember that name," he thought, as he cast a last envious look at the centurion.

How long Philostratus was gone! Solitude weighed on him, and he looked about him wildly, as though seeking some support. An attendant at this moment announced the philosopher, and Caracalla, much relieved, went into the tablinum to meet him. There he sat down on a seat in front of the writing-table strewn with tablets and papyrus-rolls, rearranged the end of the purple toga for which he had exchanged his bathing-robe, rested one foot on the lion's neck and his head on his hand. He would receive this wonderful girl in the character of an anxious sovereign meditating on the welfare of his people.

Milton Keynes UK
Ingram Content Group UK Ltd.
UKHW010628080324
438959UK00005B/365